THE HUNDRED DRESSES

ELEANOR ESTES

ILLUSTRATED BY
LOUIS SLOBODKIN

Harcourt, Inc.

ORLANDO   AUSTIN   NEW YORK   SAN DIEGO   TORONTO   LONDON

www.HarcourtBooks.com

First published 1944

Library of Congress Cataloging-in-Publication Data
Estes, Eleanor, 1906–
The hundred dresses/Eleanor Estes; illustrated by Louis Slobodkin.
p. cm.
Newbery Honor Book, 1945.
Summary: In winning a medal she is no longer there to receive,
a tight-lipped little Polish girl teaches her classmates a lesson.
Includes a note from the author's daughter, Helena Estes.
[1. Polish Americans—Fiction. 2. Friendship—Fiction.]
I. Slobodkin, Louis, 1903– ill. II. Title.
PZ7.E749Hu 2004
[Fic]—dc22 2003057037
ISBN 0-15-205170-8 ISBN 0-15-205260-7 pb

A C E G H F D B
A C E G H F D B (pb)

Manufactured in China

ALSO BY ELEANOR ESTES

Ginger Pye
(Newbery Medal Winner)

Pinky Pye

The Moffats

The Middle Moffat
(Newbery Honor Book)

Rufus M.
(Newbery Honor Book)

The Moffat Museum

The Alley

The Tunnel of Hugsy Goode

The Witch Family

A LETTER TO READERS

~

When I am asked about my mother's book *The Hundred Dresses*, I often wonder what to say. What more meaning could my words give to a book that, although written sixty years ago, continues to reach the hearts of children around the world? What answers could I give the children who still write letters of thanks and praise to my mother? "Is this a true story?" they ask. "Did this happen to you?" Well, most stories are based on both fact and fiction, and certainly this is true for *The Hundred Dresses.*

Years ago, I asked my mother why she had written the story. She told me about a classmate in her elementary school who had been taunted because she wore the same dress to school every day, and because her Polish name was unusual and difficult for many to pronounce. My mother was in school during World

War I, and Polish names were uncommon then in the small town of West Haven, Connecticut, where my mother grew up and where the story takes place. Her classmate wore the same dress to school each day because it was the only one she had. This little girl moved away to New York City in the middle of the school year, and my mother, as sometimes happens in real life, did not have the opportunity to tell her she was sorry.

My mother never forgot the little girl who had been so badly treated. She herself knew what it was like to be poor as a child, to always be cold in winter, to wear clothes passed down to her by her sister. But was this a reason to tease or be teased? Was it right to play with the feelings of one who was different?

What could she do so many years later, my mother wondered, to set things right—to reach out to the girl who had stood lonely and silent against the red brick wall of the school? Well, she thought, the one thing she could do was to write her story. And so *The Hundred Dresses* was born. Was the character Maddie based on my mother? Probably. Did Wanda really have a hundred dresses at home? Certainly in her imagination, she did.

Decades later, *The Hundred Dresses* is still loved by children. Not long ago, I received a letter from a little girl in Southern California. She was especially moved by Wanda's ability to forgive. She wrote, "Seeing people for themselves, from the inside, is one lesson I learned from Wanda. She forgave both Peggy and Maddie, even though she had to put up with them every day."

I am grateful to all the children who continue to love this extraordinary story. May *The Hundred Dresses* live on for many, many more years!

—*Helena Estes*

CONTENTS

THE HUNDRED DRESSES

WANDA

*T*ODAY, Monday, Wanda Petronski was not in her
seat. But nobody, not even Peggy and Madeline,
the girls who started all the fun, noticed her absence.

Usually Wanda sat in the next to the last seat in the

last row in Room 13. She sat in the corner of the room where the rough boys who did not make good marks on their report cards sat; the corner of the room where there was most scuffling of feet, most roars of laughter when anything funny was said, and most mud and dirt on the floor.

Wanda did not sit there because she was rough and noisy. On the contrary she was very quiet and rarely said anything at all. And nobody had ever heard her laugh out loud. Sometimes she twisted her mouth into a crooked sort of smile, but that was all.

Nobody knew exactly why Wanda sat in that seat unless it was because she came all the way from Boggins Heights, and her feet were usually caked with dry mud that she picked up coming down the country roads. Maybe the teacher liked to keep all the children who were apt to come in with dirty shoes in one corner of the room. But no one really thought much about Wanda Petronski once she was in the classroom. The time they thought about her was outside of school hours, at noontime when they were coming back to school, or in the morning early before school began, when groups of two or three or even more would be talking and laughing on their way to the school yard.

Then sometimes they waited for Wanda—to have fun with her.

The next day, Tuesday, Wanda was not in school either. And nobody noticed her absence again, except the teacher and probably big Bill Byron, who sat in the seat behind Wanda's and who could now put his long legs around her empty desk, one on each side, and sit there like a frog, to the great entertainment of all in his corner of the room.

But on Wednesday, Peggy and Maddie, who sat in the front row along with other children who got good marks and didn't track in a whole lot of mud, did notice that Wanda wasn't there. Peggy was the most popular girl in school. She was pretty; she had many pretty clothes and her auburn hair was curly. Maddie was her closest friend.

The reason Peggy and Maddie noticed Wanda's absence was because Wanda had made them late to

school. They had waited and waited for Wanda—to have some fun with her—and she just hadn't come. They kept thinking she'd come any minute. They saw Jack Beggles running to school, his necktie askew and his cap at a precarious tilt. They knew it must be late, for he always managed to slide into his chair exactly when the bell rang as though he were making a touchdown. Still they waited one minute more and one minute more, hoping she'd come. But finally they had to race off without seeing her.

The two girls reached their classroom after the doors had been closed. The children were reciting in unison the Gettysburg Address, for that was the way Miss Mason always began the session. Peggy and Maddie slipped into their seats just as the class was saying the last lines…

"that these dead shall not have died in vain; that the
nation shall, under God, have a new birth of freedom,
and that government of the people, by the people, for
the people, shall not perish from the earth."

THE DRESSES GAME

AFTER Peggy and Maddie stopped feeling like intruders in a class that had already begun, they looked across the room and noticed that Wanda was not in her seat. Furthermore her desk was dusty and looked as though she hadn't been there yesterday either. Come to think of it, they hadn't seen her yesterday. They had waited for her a little while but had forgotten about her when they reached school.

They often waited for Wanda Petronski—to have fun with her.

Wanda lived way up on Boggins Heights, and Boggins Heights was no place to live. It was a good place to go and pick wildflowers in the summer, but you always held your breath till you got safely past old man Svenson's yellow house. People in the town said old man Svenson was no good. He didn't work and, worse still, his house and yard were disgracefully dirty, with rusty tin cans strewn about and even an old straw hat. He lived alone with his dog and his cat. No wonder, said the people of the town. Who would live with him? And many stories circulated about him and the stories were the kind that made people scurry past his house even in broad daylight and hope not to meet him.

Beyond Svenson's there were a few small scattered frame houses, and in one of these Wanda Petronski lived with her father and her brother Jake.

Wanda Petronski. Most of the children in Room 13 didn't have names like that. They had names easy to say, like Thomas, Smith, or Allen. There was one boy named Bounce, Willie Bounce, and people thought that was funny but not funny in the same way that Petronski was.

Wanda didn't have any friends. She came to school alone and went home alone. She always wore a faded blue dress that didn't hang right. It was clean, but it

looked as though it had never been ironed properly. She didn't have any friends, but a lot of girls talked to her. They waited for her under the maple trees on the corner of Oliver Street. Or they surrounded her in the school yard as she stood watching some little girls play hopscotch on the worn hard ground.

"Wanda," Peggy would say in a most courteous manner, as though she were talking to Miss Mason or to the principal perhaps. "Wanda," she'd say, giving one of her friends a nudge, "tell us. How many dresses did you say you had hanging up in your closet?"

"A hundred," said Wanda.

"A hundred!" exclaimed all the girls incredulously, and the little girls would stop playing hopscotch and listen.

"Yeah, a hundred, all lined up," said Wanda. Then her thin lips drew together in silence.

"What are they like? All silk, I bet," said Peggy.

"Yeah, all silk, all colors."

"Velvet, too?"

"Yeah, velvet, too. A hundred dresses," repeated Wanda stolidly. "All lined up in my closet."

Then they'd let her go. And then before she'd gone very far, they couldn't help bursting into shrieks and peals of laughter.

A hundred dresses! Obviously the only dress Wanda had was the blue one she wore every day. So what did she say she had a hundred for? What a story! And the girls laughed derisively, while Wanda moved over to the sunny place by the ivy-covered

brick wall of the school building where she usually
stood and waited for the bell to ring.

But if the girls had met her at the corner of Oliver
Street, they'd carry her along with them for a way,

stopping every few feet for more incredulous questions. And it wasn't always dresses they talked about.
Sometimes it was hats, or coats, or even shoes.

"How many shoes did you say you had?"

"Sixty."

"Sixty! Sixty pairs or sixty shoes?"

"Sixty pairs. All lined up in my closet."

"Yesterday you said fifty."

"Now I got sixty."

Cries of exaggerated politeness greeted this.

"All alike?" said the girls.

"Oh, no. Every pair is different. All colors. All lined
up." And Wanda would shift her eyes quickly from
Peggy to a distant spot, as though she were looking far
ahead, looking but not seeing anything.

Then the outer fringe of the crowd of girls would

break away gradually, laughing, and little by little, in pairs, the group would disperse. Peggy, who had thought up this game, and Maddie, her inseparable friend, were always the last to leave. And finally Wanda would move up the street, her eyes dull and her mouth closed tight, hitching her left shoulder every now and then in the funny way she had, finishing the walk to school alone.

Peggy was not really cruel. She protected small children from bullies. And she cried for hours if she saw an animal mistreated. If anybody had said to her, "Don't you think that is a cruel way to treat Wanda?" she would have been very surprised. Cruel? What did the girl want to go and say she had a hundred dresses for? Anybody could tell that was a lie. Why did she want to lie? And she wasn't just an ordinary person, else why would she have a name like that? Anyway, they never made her cry.

As for Maddie, this business of asking Wanda every day how many dresses and how many hats and how many this and that she had was bothering her. Maddie was poor herself. She usually wore somebody's hand-me-down clothes. Thank goodness she didn't live up on Boggins Heights or have a funny name. And her forehead didn't shine the way Wanda's round one did. What did she use on it? Sapolio? That's what all the girls wanted to know.

Sometimes when Peggy was asking Wanda those questions in that mock polite voice, Maddie felt embarrassed and studied the marbles in the palm of her hand, rolling them around and saying nothing herself. Not that she felt sorry for Wanda exactly. She would never have paid any attention to Wanda if Peggy hadn't invented the dresses game. But suppose Peggy and all the others started in on her next! She wasn't as poor as Wanda perhaps, but she was poor. Of course she would have more sense than to say a hundred dresses. Still she would not like them to begin on her. Not at all! Oh, dear! She did wish Peggy would stop teasing Wanda Petronski.

A BRIGHT BLUE DAY

SOMEHOW Maddie could not buckle down to work.

She sharpened her pencil, turning it around carefully in the little red sharpener, letting the shavings fall in a neat heap on a piece of scrap paper, and trying not to get any of the dust from the lead on her clean arithmetic paper.

A slight frown puckered her forehead. In the first place she didn't like being late to school. And in the second place she kept thinking about Wanda. Somehow Wanda's desk, though empty, seemed to be the only thing she saw when she looked over to that side of the room.

How had the hundred dresses game begun in the first place? she asked herself impatiently. It was hard to remember the time when they hadn't played that game with Wanda; hard to think all the way back from now, when the hundred dresses was like the daily dozen, to then, when everything seemed much nicer. Oh, yes. She remembered. It had begun that day when Cecile first wore her new red dress. Suddenly the whole scene flashed swiftly and vividly before Maddie's eyes.

It was a bright blue day in September. No, it must have been October, because when she and Peggy were coming to school, arms around each other and singing, Peggy had said, "You know what? This must be the kind of day they mean when they say, 'October's bright blue weather.'"

Maddie remembered that because afterwards it didn't seem like bright blue weather anymore, although the weather had not changed in the slightest.

As they turned from shady Oliver Street into Maple, they both blinked. For now the morning sun shone straight in their eyes. Besides that, bright flashes of color came from a group of a half dozen or more girls across the street. Their sweaters and jackets and dresses, blues and golds and reds, and one crimson one in particular, caught the sun's rays like bright pieces of glass.

A crisp, fresh wind was blowing, swishing their skirts and blowing their hair in their eyes. The girls were all exclaiming and shouting and each one was trying to talk louder than the others. Maddie and Peggy joined the group, and the laughing, and the talking.

"Hi, Peg! Hi, Maddie!" they were greeted warmly. "Look at Cecile!"

What they were all exclaiming about was the dress that Cecile had on—a crimson dress with cap and socks to match. It was a bright new dress and very pretty. Everyone was admiring it and admiring Cecile. For long, slender Cecile was a toe dancer and wore fancier clothes than most of them. And she had her black satin bag with her precious white satin ballet slippers slung over her shoulders. Today was the day for her dancing lesson.

Maddie sat down on the granite curbstone to tie her shoelaces. She listened happily to what they were saying. They all seemed especially jolly today, probably because it was such a bright day. Everything sparkled. Way down at the end of the street the sun shimmered and turned to silver the blue water of the bay. Maddie picked up a piece of broken mirror and flashed a small circle of light edged with rainbow colors onto the houses, the trees, and the top of the telegraph pole.

And it was then that Wanda had come along with her brother Jake.

They didn't often come to school together. Jake had to get to school very early because he helped old Mr. Heany, the school janitor, with the furnace, or raking up the dry leaves, or other odd jobs before school opened. Today he must be late.

Even Wanda looked pretty in this sunshine, and her pale blue dress looked like a piece of the sky in summer; and that old gray toboggan cap she wore—it must be something Jake had found—looked almost jaunty. Maddie watched them absentmindedly as she flashed her piece of broken mirror here and there. And only absentmindedly she noticed Wanda stop short when they reached the crowd of laughing and shouting girls.

"Come on," Maddie heard Jake say. "I gotta hurry. I gotta get the doors open and ring the bell."

"You go the rest of the way," said Wanda. "I want to stay here."

Jake shrugged and went on up Maple Street. Wanda slowly approached the group of girls. With each step forward, before she put her foot down she seemed to hesitate for a long, long time. She approached the group as a timid animal might, ready to run if anything alarmed it.

Even so, Wanda's mouth was twisted into the vaguest suggestion of a smile. She must feel happy, too, because everybody must feel happy on such a day.

As Wanda joined the outside fringe of girls, Maddie stood up, too, and went over close to Peggy to get a good look at Cecile's new dress herself. She forgot about Wanda, and more girls kept coming up, enlarging the group and all exclaiming about Cecile's new dress.

"Isn't it lovely!" said one.

"Yeah, I have a new blue dress, but it's not as pretty as that," said another.

"My mother just bought me a plaid, one of the Stuart plaids."

"I got a new dress for dancing school."

"I'm gonna make my mother get me one just like Cecile's."

Everyone was talking to everybody else. Nobody said anything to Wanda, but there she was, a part of the crowd. The girls closed in a tighter circle around Cecile, still talking all at once and admiring her, and Wanda was somehow enveloped in the group. Nobody talked to Wanda, but nobody even thought about her being there.

Maybe, thought Maddie, remembering what had happened next, maybe she figured all she'd have to do was say something and she'd really be one of the girls. And this would be an easy thing to do because all they were doing was talking about dresses.

Maddie was standing next to Peggy. Wanda was

standing next to Peggy on the other side. All of a sudden, Wanda impulsively touched Peggy's arm and said something. Her light blue eyes were shining and she looked excited like the rest of the girls.

"What?" asked Peggy. For Wanda had spoken very softly.

Wanda hesitated a moment and then she repeated her words firmly.

"I got a hundred dresses home."

"That's what I thought you said. A hundred dresses. A hundred!" Peggy's voice raised itself higher and higher.

"Hey, kids!" she yelled. "This girl's got a hundred dresses."

Silence greeted this, and the crowd which had centered around Cecile and her new finery now centered curiously around Wanda and Peggy. The girls eyed Wanda, first incredulously, then suspiciously.

"A hundred dresses?" they said. "Nobody could have a hundred dresses."

"I have though."

"Wanda has a hundred dresses."

"Where are they then?"

"In my closet."

"Oh, you don't wear them to school."

"No. For parties."

"Oh, you mean you don't have any everyday dresses."

"Yes, I have all kinds of dresses."

"Why don't you wear them to school?"

For a moment Wanda was silent to this. Her lips drew together. Then she repeated stolidly as though it were a lesson learned in school, "A hundred of them. All lined up in my closet."

"Oh, I see," said Peggy, talking like a grown-up person. "The child has a hundred dresses, but she wouldn't wear them to school. Perhaps she's worried of getting ink or chalk on them."

With this everybody fell to laughing and talking at once. Wanda looked stolidly at them, pursing her lips together, wrinkling her forehead up so that the gray toboggan slipped way down on her brow. Suddenly from down the street the school gong rang its first warning.

"Oh, come on, hurry," said Maddie, relieved. "We'll be late."

"Good-bye, Wanda," said Peggy. "Your hundred dresses sound bee-you-tiful."

More shouts of laughter greeted this, and off the girls ran, laughing and talking and forgetting Wanda and her hundred dresses. Forgetting until tomorrow and the next day and the next, when Peggy, seeing her coming to school, would remember and ask her about the hundred dresses. For now Peggy seemed to think a day was lost if she had not had some fun with Wanda, winning the approving laughter of the girls.

Yes, that was the way it had all begun, the game of the hundred dresses. It all happened so suddenly and unexpectedly, with everybody falling right in, that even if you felt uncomfortable as Maddie had there wasn't anything you could do about it. Maddie wagged her head up and down. Yes, she repeated to herself, that was the way it began, that day, that bright blue day.

And she wrapped up her shavings and went to the front of the room to empty them in the teacher's basket.

THE CONTEST

NOW today, even though she and Peggy had been late to school, Maddie was glad she had not had to make fun of Wanda. She worked her arithmetic problems absentmindedly. Eight times eight...

let's see…nothing she could do about making fun of Wanda. She wished she had the nerve to write Peggy a note, because she knew she'd never have the courage to speak right out to Peggy, to say, "Hey, Peg, let's stop asking Wanda how many dresses she has."

When she finished her arithmetic, she did start a note to Peggy. Suddenly she paused and shuddered. She pictured herself in the school yard, a new target for Peggy and the girls. Peggy might ask her where she got the dress she had on, and Maddie would have to say that it was one of Peggy's old ones that Maddie's mother had tried to disguise with new trimmings so that no one in Room 13 would recognize it.

If only Peggy would decide of her own accord to stop having fun with Wanda. Oh, well! Maddie ran her hand through her short blond hair as though to push the uncomfortable thoughts away. What difference did it make? Slowly Maddie tore the note she had started into bits. She was Peggy's best friend, and Peggy was the best-liked girl in the whole room. Peggy could not possibly do anything that was really wrong, she thought.

As for Wanda, she was just some girl who lived up on Boggins Heights and stood alone in the school yard. Nobody in the room thought about Wanda at all except when it was her turn to stand up for oral reading. Then they all hoped she would hurry up and finish and sit down, because it took her forever to read a paragraph. Sometimes she stood up and just looked at her book and couldn't, or wouldn't, read at all. The teacher tried to help her, but she'd just stand there until the teacher told her to sit down. Was she dumb or what?

Maybe she was just timid. The only time she talked was in the school yard about her hundred dresses. Maddie remembered her telling about one of her dresses, a pale blue one with cerise-colored trimmings. And she remembered another that was brilliant jungle green with a red sash. "You'd look like a Christmas tree in that," the girls had said in pretended admiration.

Thinking about Wanda and her hundred dresses all lined up in the closet, Maddie began to wonder who was going to win the drawing and color contest. For girls, this contest consisted of designing dresses, and for boys, of designing motorboats. Probably Peggy would win the girls' medal. Peggy drew better than anyone else in the room. At least that's what everybody thought. You should see the way she could copy a picture in a magazine or some film star's head. You could almost tell who it was. Oh, Maddie did hope Peggy would win. Hope so? She was sure Peggy would win. Well, tomorrow the teacher was going to announce the winners. Then they'd know.

Thoughts of Wanda sank further and further from Maddie's mind, and by the time the history lesson began she had forgotten all about her.

THE HUNDRED DRESSES

THE next day it was drizzling. Maddie and Peggy hurried to school under Peggy's umbrella. Naturally on a day like this they didn't wait for Wanda Petronski on the corner of Oliver Street, the street that far, far away, under the railroad tracks and up the hill, led to Boggins Heights. Anyway they weren't taking chances on being late today, because today was important.

"Do you think Miss Mason will surely announce the winners today?" asked Peggy.

"Oh, I hope so, the minute we get in," said Maddie, and added, "Of course you'll win, Peg."

"Hope so," said Peggy eagerly.

The minute they entered the classroom they stopped short and gasped. There were drawings all over the room, on every ledge and windowsill, tacked to the tops of the blackboards, spread over the bird charts, dazzling colors and brilliant lavish designs, all drawn on great sheets of wrapping paper.

There must have been a hundred of them all lined up!

These must be the drawings for the contest. They

were! Everybody stopped and whistled or murmured admiringly.

As soon as the class had assembled Miss Mason announced the winners. Jack Beggles had won for the boys, she said, and his design of an outboard motorboat was on exhibition in Room 12, along with the sketches by all the other boys.

"As for the girls," she said, "although just one or two sketches were submitted by most, one girl—and Room 13 should be very proud of her—this one girl actually drew one hundred designs—all different and all beautiful. In the opinion of the judges, any one of her drawings is worthy of winning the prize. I am happy to say that Wanda Petronski is the winner of the girls' medal. Unfortunately Wanda has been absent from school for some days and is not here to receive the applause that is due her. Let us hope she will be back tomorrow. Now, class, you may file around the room quietly and look at her exquisite drawings."

The children burst into applause, and even the boys were glad to have a chance to stamp on the floor, put their fingers in their mouths and whistle, though they were not interested in dresses. Maddie and Peggy were among the first to reach the blackboard to look at the drawings.

"Look, Peg," whispered Maddie, "there's that blue one she told us about. Isn't it beautiful?"

"Yeah," said Peggy, "and here's that green one. Boy, and I thought I could draw!"

While the class was circling the room, the monitor from the principal's office brought Miss Mason a note. Miss Mason read it several times and studied it thoughtfully for a while. Then she clapped her hands and said, "Attention, class. Everyone back to his seat."

When the shuffling of feet had stopped and the room was still and quiet, Miss Mason said, "I have a letter from Wanda's father that I want to read to you."

Miss Mason stood there a moment and the silence in the room grew tense and expectant. The teacher adjusted her glasses slowly and deliberately. Her manner indicated that what was coming—this letter from Wanda's father—was a matter of great importance. Everybody listened closely as Miss Mason read the brief note:

"Dear teacher: My Wanda will not come to your school anymore. Jake also. Now we move away to big city. No more holler Polack. No more ask why funny name. Plenty of funny names in the big city.

Yours truly, Jan Petronski."

A deep silence met the reading of this letter. Miss Mason took her glasses off, blew on them, and wiped them on her soft white handkerchief. Then she put them on again and looked at the class. When she spoke her voice was very low.

"I am sure none of my boys and girls in Room 13 would purposely and deliberately hurt anyone's feelings because his name happened to be a long, unfamiliar one. I prefer to think that what was said was said in thoughtlessness. I know that all of you feel the way I do, that this is a very unfortunate thing to have happen. Unfortunate and sad, both. And I want you all to think about it."

The first period was a study period. Maddie tried to prepare her lessons, but she could not put her mind on her work. She had a very sick feeling in the bottom of her stomach. True, she had not enjoyed listening to Peggy ask Wanda how many dresses she had in her closet, but she had said nothing. She had stood by silently, and that was just as bad as what Peggy had done. Worse. She was a coward. At least Peggy hadn't considered they were being mean, but she, Maddie, had thought they were doing wrong. She had thought, supposing she was the one being made fun of. She could put herself in Wanda's shoes. But she had done just as much as Peggy to make life miserable for Wanda by simply standing by and saying nothing. She had helped to make someone so unhappy that she had had to move away from town.

Goodness! Wasn't there anything she could do? If only she could tell Wanda she hadn't meant to hurt her feelings. She turned around and stole a glance at Peggy,

but Peggy did not look up. She seemed to be studying hard.

Well, whether Peggy felt badly or not, she, Maddie, had to do something. She had to find Wanda Petronski. Maybe she had not yet moved away. Maybe Peggy would climb the Heights with her and they would tell Wanda she had won the contest. And that they thought she was smart and the hundred dresses were beautiful.

When school was dismissed in the afternoon, Peggy said with pretended casualness, "Hey, let's go and see if that kid has left town or not."

So Peggy had had the same idea as Maddie had had! Maddie glowed. Peggy was really all right, just as she always thought. Peg was really all right. She was okay.

UP ON BOGGINS HEIGHTS

*T*HE two girls hurried out of the building, up the street toward Boggins Heights, the part of town that wore such a forbidding air on this kind of November afternoon, drizzly, damp, and dismal.

"Well, at least," said Peggy gruffly, "I never did call

her a foreigner or make fun of her name. I never thought she had the sense to know we were making fun of her anyway. I thought she was too dumb. And, gee, look how she can draw! And I thought I could draw."

Maddie could say nothing. All she hoped was that they would find Wanda. Just so she'd be able to tell her they were sorry they had all picked on her. And just to say how wonderful the whole school thought she was, and please not to move away and everybody would be nice. She and Peggy would fight anybody who was not nice.

Maddie fell to imagining a story in which she and Peggy assailed any bully who might be going to pick on Wanda. "Petronski—Onski!" somebody would yell, and she and Peggy would pounce on the guilty one. For a time Maddie consoled herself with these thoughts, but they soon vanished and again she felt unhappy and wished everything could be nice the way it was before any of them had made fun of Wanda.

Br-r-r! How drab and cold and cheerless it was up here on the Heights! In the summertime the woods, the sumac, and the ferns that grew along the brook on the side of the road were lush and made this a beautiful walk on Sunday afternoons. But now it did not seem beautiful. The brook had shrunk to the merest trickle, and today's drizzle sharpened the outlines of the rusty tin cans, old shoes, and forlorn remnants of a big black umbrella in the bed of the brook.

The two girls hurried on. They hoped to get to the top of the hill before dark. Otherwise they were not certain they could find Wanda's house. At last, puffing and panting, they rounded the top of the hill. The first house, that old rickety one, belonged to old man Svenson. Peggy and Maddie hurried past it almost on tiptoe. Somebody said once that old man Svenson had shot a man. Others said, "Nonsense! He's an old good-for-nothing. Wouldn't hurt a flea."

But, false or not, the girls breathed more freely as they rounded the corner. It was too cold and drizzly for old man Svenson to be in his customary chair tilted against the house, chewing and spitting tobacco juice. Even his dog was nowhere in sight and had not barked at the girls from wherever he might be.

"I think that's where the Petronkis live," said Maddie, pointing to a little white house with lots of chicken coops at the side of it. Wisps of old grass stuck up here and there along the pathway like thin wet kittens. The house and its sparse little yard looked shabby

but clean. It reminded Maddie of Wanda's one dress, her faded blue cotton dress, shabby but clean.

There was not a sign of life about the house except for a yellow cat, half grown, crouching on the one small step close to the front door. It leapt timidly with a small cry halfway up a tree when the girls came into the yard. Peggy knocked firmly on the door, but there was no answer. She and Maddie went around to the backyard and knocked there. Still there was no answer.

"Wanda!" called Peggy. They listened sharply, but only a deep silence pressed against their eardrums. There was no doubt about it. The Petronskis were gone.

"Maybe they just went away for a little while and haven't really left with their furniture yet," suggested Maddie hopefully. Maddie was beginning to wonder

how she could bear the hard fact that Wanda had
actually gone and that she might never be able to make
amends.

"Well," said Peggy, "let's see if the door is open."

They cautiously turned the knob of the front door.
It opened easily, for it was a light thing and looked as
though it furnished but frail protection against the cold
winds that blew up here in the wintertime. The little
square room that the door opened into was empty.
There was absolutely nothing left in it, and in the
corner a closet with its door wide open was empty,
too. Maddie wondered what it had held before the
Petronskis moved out. And she thought of Wanda
saying, "Sure, a hundred dresses...all lined up in the
closet."

Well, anyway, real and imaginary dresses alike were

gone. The Petronskis were gone. And now how could she and Peggy tell Wanda anything? Maybe the teacher knew where she had moved to. Maybe old man Svenson knew. They might knock on his door and ask on the way down. Or the post office might know. If they wrote a letter, Wanda might get it because the post office might forward it. Feeling very downcast and discouraged, the girls closed the door and started for home. Coming down the road, way, way off in the distance, through the drizzle they could see the water of the bay, gray and cold.

"Do you suppose that was their cat and they forgot her?" asked Peggy. But the cat wasn't anywhere around now, and as the girls turned the bend they saw her crouching under the dilapidated wooden chair in front of old man Svenson's house. So perhaps the cat belonged to him. They lost their courage about knocking on his door and asking when the Petronskis had left and anyway, goodness! here was old man Svenson himself coming up the road. Everything about Svenson was yellow; his house, his cat, his trousers, his drooping mustache and tangled hair, his hound loping behind him, and the long streams of tobacco juice he expertly shot from between his scattered yellow teeth. The two girls drew over to the side of the path as they hurried by. When they were a good way past, they stopped.

"Hey, Mr. Svenson!" yelled Peggy. "When did the Petronskis move?"

Old man Svenson turned around, but said nothing. Finally he did answer, but his words were unintelligible, and the two girls turned and ran down the hill as fast as they could. Old man Svenson looked after them for a moment and then went on up the hill, muttering to himself and scratching his head.

When they were back down on Oliver Street again, the girls stopped running. They still felt disconsolate, and Maddie wondered if she were going to be unhappy about Wanda and the hundred dresses forever. Nothing would ever seem good to her again, because just when she was about to enjoy something—like going for a hike with Peggy to look for bayberries or sliding down Barley Hill—she'd bump right smack into the thought that she had made Wanda Petronski move away.

"Well, anyway," said Peggy, "she's gone now, so what can we do? Besides, when I was asking her about all of her dresses she probably was getting good ideas for her drawings. She might not even have won the contest otherwise."

Maddie carefully turned this idea over in her head, for if there were anything in it she would not have to feel so bad. But that night she could not get to sleep. She thought about Wanda and her faded blue dress and the little house she had lived in; and old man Svenson living a few steps away. And she thought of the glowing picture those hundred dresses made—all lined up in the classroom.

At last Maddie sat up in bed and pressed her

forehead tight in her hands and really thought. This was the hardest thinking she had ever done. After a long, long time she reached an important conclusion.

She was never going to stand by and say nothing again.

If she ever heard anybody picking on someone because they were funny looking or because they had strange names, she'd speak up. Even if it meant losing Peggy's friendship. She had no way of making things right with Wanda, but from now on she would never make anybody else so unhappy again. Finally, all tired out, Maddie fell asleep.

THE LETTER TO ROOM 13

O N Saturday Maddie spent the afternoon with Peggy. They were writing a letter to Wanda Petronski.

It was just a friendly letter telling about the contest and telling Wanda she had won. They told her how pretty her drawings were, and that now they were studying about Winfield Scott in school. And they asked her if she liked where she was living now and if she liked her new teacher. They had meant to say they were sorry, but it ended up with their just writing a friendly letter, the kind they would have written to any good friend, and they signed it with lots of X's for love.

They mailed the letter to Boggins Heights, writing "Please Forward" on the envelope. The teacher had not known where Wanda had moved to, so their only hope was that the post office knew. The minute they dropped the letter in the mailbox they both felt happier and more carefree.

Days passed and there was no answer, but the letter did not come back so maybe Wanda had received it.

Perhaps she was so hurt and angry she was not going to answer. You could not blame her. And Maddie remembered the way she hitched her left shoulder up as she walked off to school alone, and how the girls always said, "Why does her dress always hang funny like that, and why does she wear those queer, high, laced shoes?"

They knew she didn't have any mother, but they hadn't thought about it. They hadn't thought she had to do her own washing and ironing. She only had one dress and she must have had to wash and iron it overnight. Maybe sometimes it wasn't dry when it was time to put it on in the morning. But it was always clean.

Several weeks went by and still Wanda did not answer. Peggy had begun to forget the whole business, and Maddie put herself to sleep at night making speeches about Wanda, defending her from great

crowds of girls who were trying to tease her with, "How many dresses have you got?" Before Wanda could press her lips together in a tight line the way she did before answering, Maddie would cry out, "Stop! This girl is just a girl just like you are…" And then everybody would feel ashamed the way she used to feel. Sometimes she rescued Wanda from a sinking ship or the hoofs of a runaway horse. "Oh, that's all right," she'd say when Wanda thanked her with dull pained eyes.

Now it was Christmastime and there was snow on
the ground. Christmas bells and a small tree decorated
the classroom. And on one narrow blackboard Jack
Beggles had drawn a jolly fat Santa Claus in red and
white chalk. On the last day of school before the holi-
days, the children in Peggy and Maddie's class had a
Christmas party. The teacher's desk was rolled back

and a piano rolled in. First the children had acted the story of Tiny Tim. Then they had sung songs and Cecile had done some dances in different costumes. The dance called the "Passing of Autumn," in which she whirled and spun like a red and golden autumn leaf, was the favorite.

After the party the teacher said she had a surprise, and she showed the class a letter she had received that morning.

"Guess who this is from," she said. "You remember Wanda Petronski? The bright little artist who won the drawing contest? Well, she has written me and I am glad to know where she lives because now I can send her medal. And I hope it gets there for Christmas. I want to read her letter to you."

The class sat up with a sudden interest, and listened intently to Miss Mason as she read the letter.

"Dear Miss Mason:

How are you and Room 13? Please tell the girls they can keep those hundred dresses because in my new house I have a hundred new ones all lined up in my closet. I'd like that girl Peggy to have the drawing of the green dress with the red trimming and her friend Maddie to have the blue one. For Christmas. I miss that school and my new teacher does not equalize with you. Merry Christmas to you and everybody.

Yours truly, Wanda Petronski."

The teacher passed the letter around the room for everybody to see. It was pretty, decorated with a picture of a Christmas tree lighted up in the night in a park surrounded by high buildings.

On the way home from school Maddie and Peggy held their drawings very carefully. They had stayed late to help straighten up after the play and it was getting dark. The houses looked warm and inviting with wreaths and holly and lighted trees in their windows. Outside the grocery store hundreds of Christmas trees were stacked, and in the window candy peppermint canes and cornucopias of shiny bright transparent paper were strung. The air smelled like Christmas and bright lights everywhere reflected different colors on the snow.

"The colors are like the colors in Wanda's hundred dresses," said Maddie.

"Yes," said Peggy, holding her drawing out to look at it under the street lamp. "And boy! This shows she really liked us. It shows she got our letter and this is her way of saying that everything's all right. And that's that," she said with finality.

Peggy felt happy and relieved. It was Christmas and everything was fine.

"I hope so," said Maddie sadly. She felt sad because she knew she would never see the little tight-lipped Polish girl again and couldn't ever really make things right between them.

She went home and she pinned her drawing over a torn place in the pink-flowered wallpaper in the bedroom. The shabby room came alive from the brilliancy of the colors. Maddie sat down on the edge of her bed and looked at the drawing. She had stood by and said nothing, but Wanda had been nice to her anyway.

Tears blurred her eyes and she gazed for a long time at the picture. Then hastily she rubbed her eyes and studied it intently. The colors in the dress were so vivid she had scarcely noticed the face and head of the drawing. But it looked like her, Maddie! It really did. The same short blond hair, blue eyes, and wide straight mouth. Why, it really looked like her own self! Wanda had really drawn this for her. Wanda had drawn her! In excitement she ran over to Peggy's.

"Peg!" she said. "Let me see your picture."

"What's the matter?" asked Peggy as they clattered up the stairs to her room, where Wanda's drawing was lying facedown on the bed. Maddie carefully lifted it up.

"Look! She drew you. That's you!" she exclaimed. And the head and face of this picture did look like the auburn-haired Peggy.

"What did I say!" said Peggy. "She must have really liked us anyway."

"Yes, she must have," agreed Maddie, and she blinked away the tears that came every time she thought of Wanda standing alone in that sunny spot in the school yard close to the wall, looking stolidly over at the group of laughing girls after she had walked off, after she had said, "Sure, a hundred of them—all lined up..."